THOMAS & FRIENDS

Kevin Meets Cranky

Cranky was having a busy day at the Docks. He worked as **hard** as he could, but still more cargo arrived.

"Lifting and loading, does it ever stop?" he moaned, as boxes piled up around him.

The Fat Controller asked Kevin to help Cranky.

Kevin was very excited. "I've always wanted to meet Cranky!" he smiled.

He couldn't wait to show everyone what a Really Useful Crane he was!

"Hello, Cranky," said Kevin when he arrived. "I'm here to lend a helping hook. What do you want me to do?"

"I don't need any help," Cranky replied.

"But surely there's **something** I can do?" Kevin asked.

"Stay out of my way!" said Cranky. "I don't need **any** help thank you very much."

Then, as Cranky
unloaded pipes from
a ship, some got loose.

"Look out!" he yelled,
as they crashed down
onto the Docks.

"I'll get them!" Kevin called,
as he rushed to help.

Kevin stacked up all the pipes as neatly as he could.

"There you go, Cranky. All done!" he said.

But Cranky wasn't happy. "That was **your** fault!" he said. "Watching me all the time. You're making me nervous. Go away and stop interfering!"

Later, when Cranky was carrying a crate of chickens, it cracked open and they escaped!

"Don't worry, all under control!" Kevin said, collecting up the chickens.

"I told you to stay out of my way!" Cranky replied. "All your whizzing around is making me **dizzy!**"

Then Kevin heard a **crash** as Cranky's hook knocked over some barrels, sending one rolling towards the sea.

Kevin rushed to stop it. "I've got it," he said as he reached the barrel, but he couldn't stop and fell into the sea!

"Help! Help!" called Kevin.

"Crane overboard!" Salty shouted.

Cranky quickly lowered his hook and carefully lifted Kevin out of the sea.

"Well done, matey!" smiled Salty.

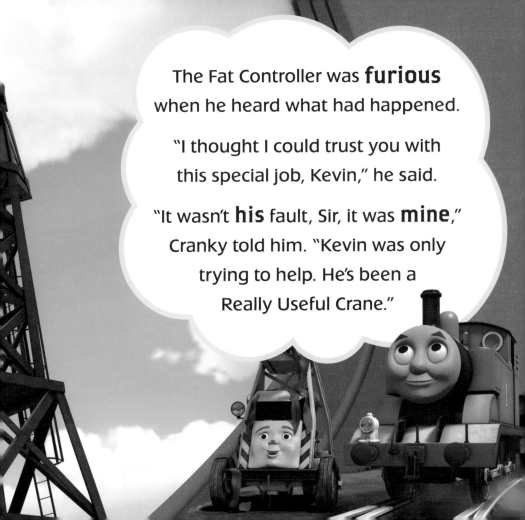

The Fat Controller was **furious** when he heard what had happened.

"I thought I could trust you with this special job, Kevin," he said.

"It wasn't **his** fault, Sir, it was **mine**," Cranky told him. "Kevin was only trying to help. He's been a Really Useful Crane."

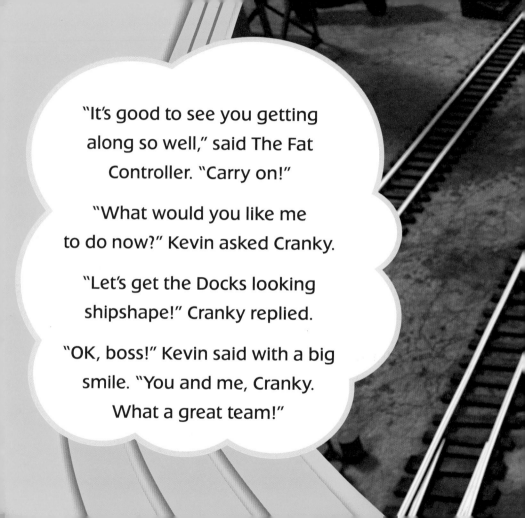

"It's good to see you getting along so well," said The Fat Controller. "Carry on!"

"What would you like me to do now?" Kevin asked Cranky.

"Let's get the Docks looking shipshape!" Cranky replied.

"OK, boss!" Kevin said with a big smile. "You and me, Cranky. What a great team!"